KITES

Magic Wishes That Fly Up to the Sky

Demi

DRAGONFLY BOOKS® • CROWN PUBLISHERS
New York

For
Lian-sheng   Sheng-yen Lu

DRAGONFLY BOOKS® PUBLISHED BY CROWN PUBLISHERS

Published by Crown Publishers, a division of Random House, Inc.,
1540 Broadway, New York, NY 10036

www.randomhouse.com/kids

Library of Congress Cataloging-in-Publication Data

Demi.

Kites : magic wishes that fly up to the sky / Demi.

p. cm.

1. Kites—Juvenile literature. I. Title.

TL759.5.D46   1999

394.26951—dc21   98-41372

ISBN 0-517-80049-7 (trade)
ISBN 0-517-80050-0 (lib. bdg.)
ISBN 0-375-81008-0 (pbk.)

First Dragonfly Books® edition: December 2000

Printed in the United States of America

10 9 8 7 6 5 4 3 2 1

Once upon a time,

and long ago in China,

there lived a painter of holy pictures.

Many people would buy his pictures

and offer them in the temple

to their gods.

They hoped and prayed their wishes would come true. For example, if somebody wanted to be smart, he would offer a picture of Manjushri, the God of Wisdom. If somebody wanted money, he would offer a picture of an abacus, which was used for counting money.

If somebody wanted peace, he would offer a picture of the Peaceful Buddha. If somebody had bad eyesight and wanted good eyesight, he would offer a picture of himself without his glasses on.

One day, a local woman came to the painter. She said, "I want a picture of a dragon, the symbol of wealth, wisdom, power, and nobility, so that my son will grow up big and strong. But I do not want an ordinary picture. I want you to paint it as a kite with strings. Then I can fly it right up to the sky and the gods in heaven will see it immediately, instead of having to come down to this temple."

The man painted a marvelous dragon kite for the
woman, which she immediately flew to the heavens.
Her son helped with the strings, and already he
seemed bigger and stronger, richer and nobler,
to everyone who saw him.

And so the other villagers went to the painter asking for their offerings to be painted on kites, too. They asked for many wishes for their children, their parents, their husbands or wives, and for themselves. The holy painter was so busy painting kite after kite that he hardly had any time to paint holy pictures.

Eagle represents power and success.

Mandarin Duck means nobility, faithfulness, and happiness.

Egret, for good luck.

Wild Goose, for brightness, power, and harmony.

They asked for birds.

Magpie to bring joy.

Thin Swallow, for female loveliness.

The Phoenix, for happiness, peace, luck, kindness, compassion, and glory.

Fat Swallow symbolizes male greatness, innocence, and peace.

Crane stands for nobility and honesty.

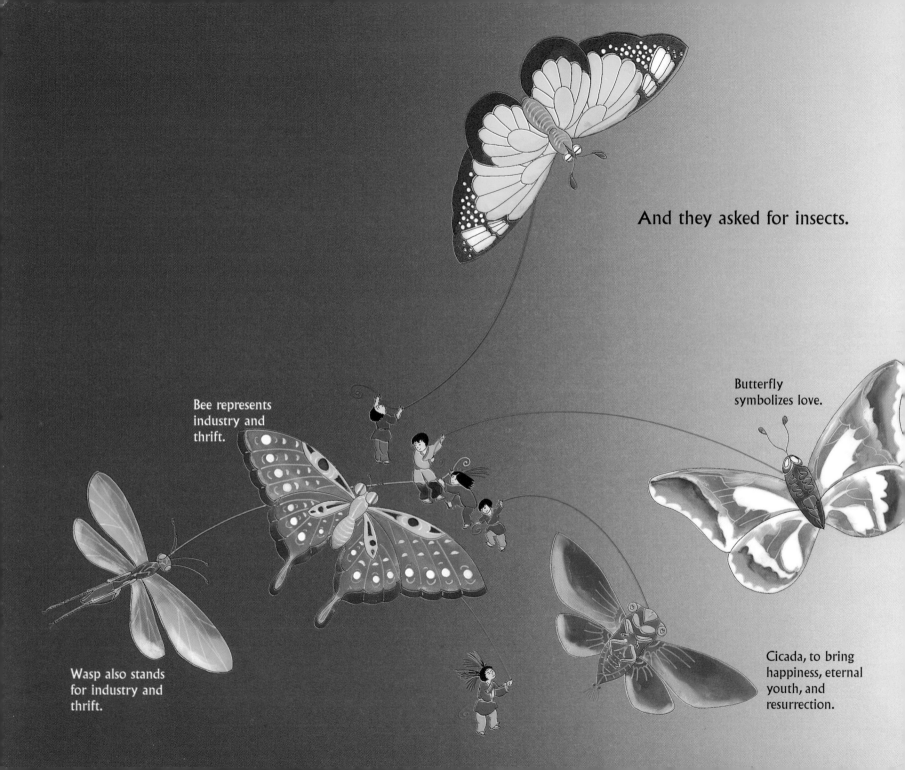

And they asked for insects.

Bee represents
industry and
thrift.

Wasp also stands
for industry and
thrift.

Butterfly
symbolizes love.

Cicada, to bring
happiness, eternal
youth, and
resurrection.

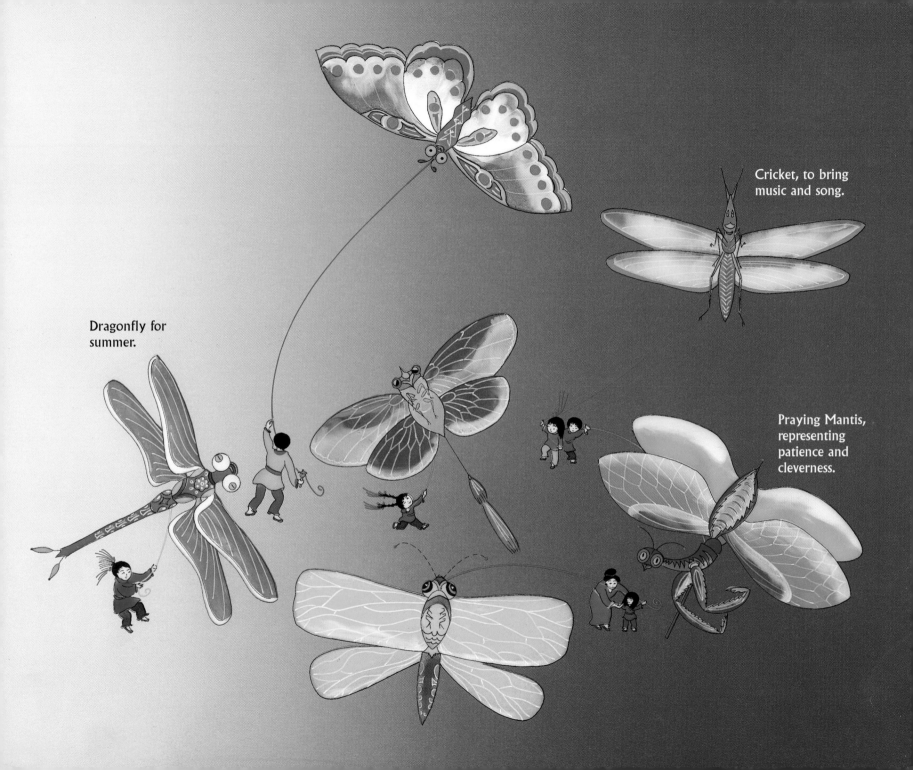

Cricket, to bring music and song.

Dragonfly for summer.

Praying Mantis, representing patience and cleverness.

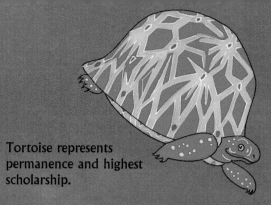

Tortoise represents permanence and highest scholarship.

The people requested kites that looked like reptiles, fish, and crustaceans.

Crab helps to repel bad omens.

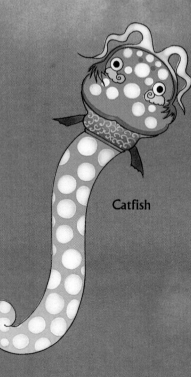

Catfish

Goldfish brings happiness, wealth, and wisdom.

Frog symbolizes long life and joy.

Lizard, for quickness and cleverness.

Tadpole symbolizes wealth and protection.

Carp is for abundance.

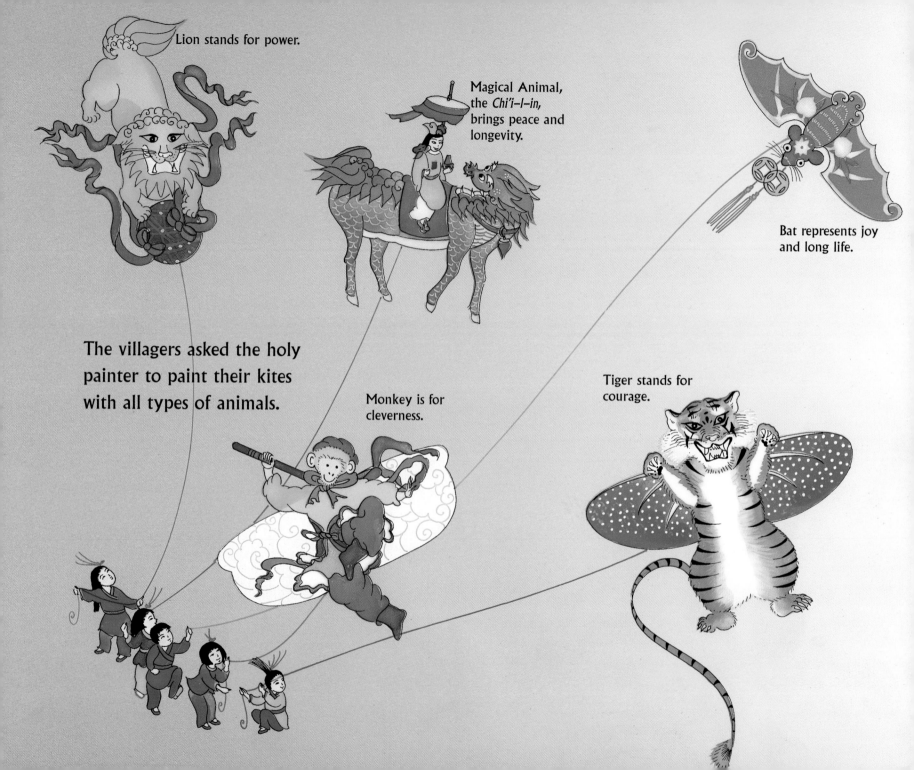

Lion stands for power.

Magical Animal, the *Chi'i-l-in,* brings peace and longevity.

Bat represents joy and long life.

The villagers asked the holy painter to paint their kites with all types of animals.

Monkey is for cleverness.

Tiger stands for courage.

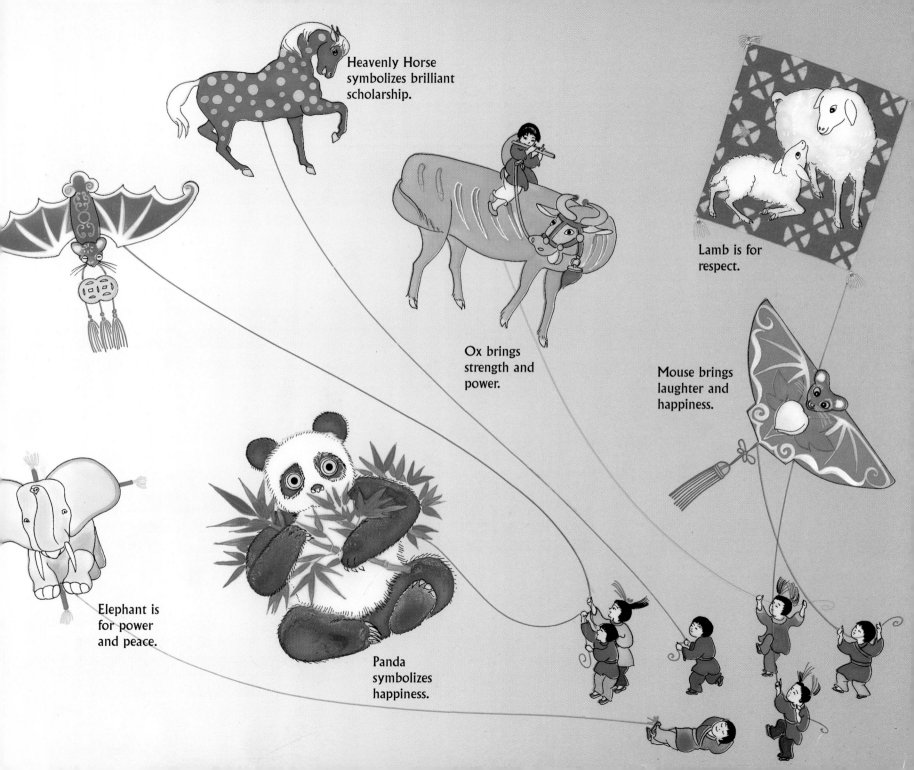

Heavenly Horse symbolizes brilliant scholarship.

Lamb is for respect.

Ox brings strength and power.

Mouse brings laughter and happiness.

Elephant is for power and peace.

Panda symbolizes happiness.

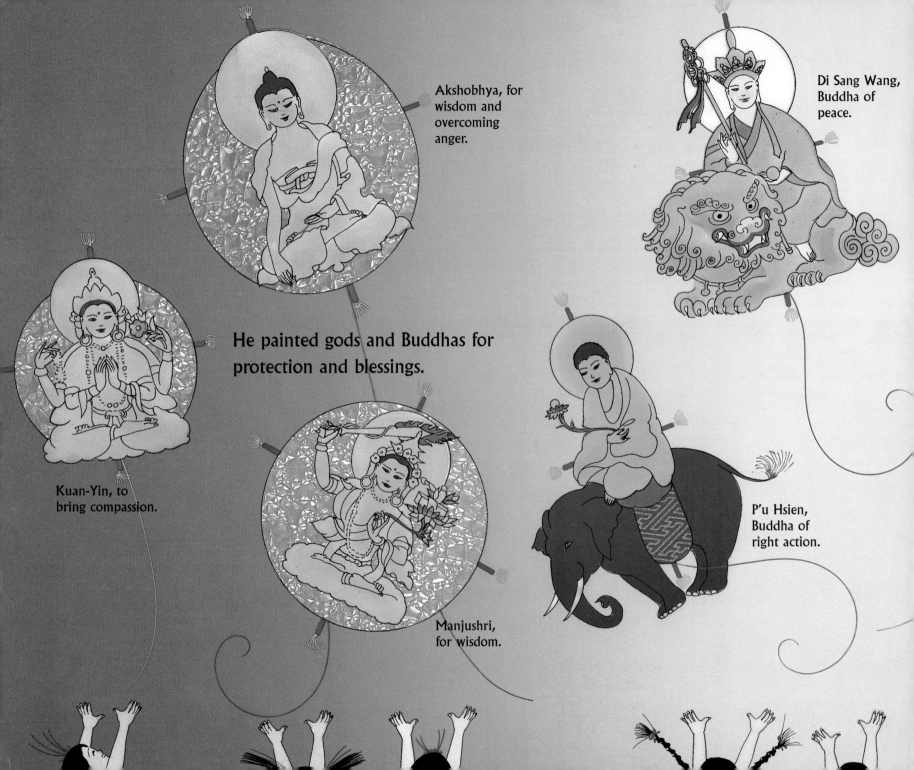

Akshobhya, for wisdom and overcoming anger.

Di Sang Wang, Buddha of peace.

Kuan-Yin, to bring compassion.

He painted gods and Buddhas for protection and blessings.

Manjushri, for wisdom.

P'u Hsien, Buddha of right action.

Amitabha, the
Buddha of light,
to overcome
greed.

Amoghasiddhi, the
Buddha of wisdom,
to overcome
jealousy.

The Jade
Emperor, for
power.

Vairochana, the
teaching Buddha.

Vajrapani, Buddha
of protection, to
overcome evil.

Ratnasambhava, the
Buddha of equality, to
overcome ego.

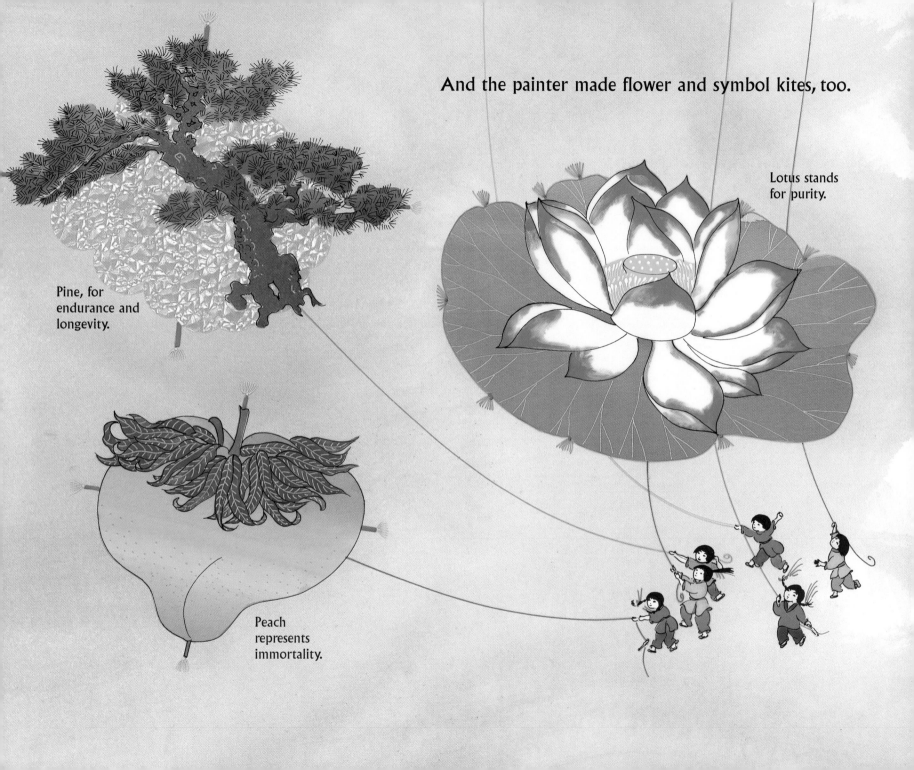

And the painter made flower and symbol kites, too.

Lotus stands
for purity.

Pine, for
endurance and
longevity.

Peach
represents
immortality.

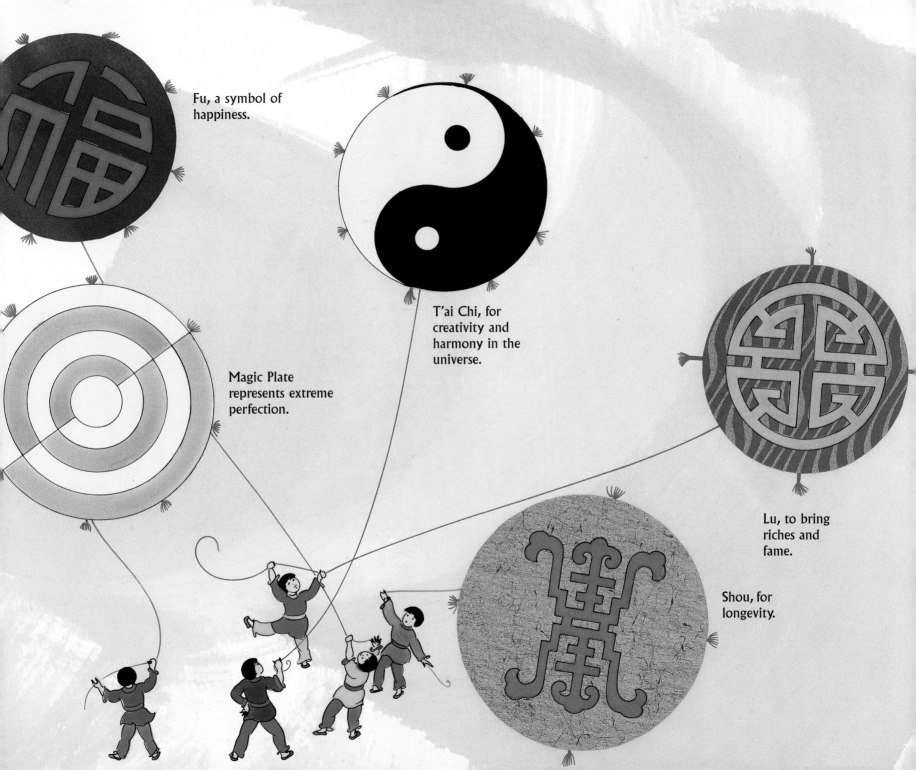

Fu, a symbol of happiness.

T'ai Chi, for creativity and harmony in the universe.

Magic Plate represents extreme perfection.

Lu, to bring riches and fame.

Shou, for longevity.

In addition to asking for wishes, many people used their kites to send off bad luck.

They would let their kite strings out as far as they could go and then cut the strings, sending the bad luck away.

As the kite drifted far away with the wind, all disease and calamities were carried away, too.

Later on in China, these magic kites took on an even deeper meaning and developed into a festival of kites called *The Double Ninth Festival* (Ch'ing Yang), held on the ninth day of the ninth month: September 9th.

When the chrysanthemum, or flower of autumn, blooms, families celebrate by climbing up to the highest hills, having picnics, and flying their kites.

On this day, kite-flying is taken as a symbol of rising higher and higher, being better and better, stronger, smarter, and finer in everything one does.

All kinds of kites drift and dance in the clear, boundless space and compete with each other in contests of endurance, originality, and beauty.

The contests begin, with either solo flyers or kite-flying teams taking part, and kites of every size and shape rise up to the sky—huge kites and tiny kites, some only inches long.

Some have sharp two-bladed knives attached to the string to cut the other kites down, and some have strings that have been treated with powdered glass. The treated strings can cut the strings of the other kites, causing them to somersault and fall.

Some kites have whistles that sing in the sky; some have a gong and drum attached; others have blinking eyes. Decorations help bring luck and happiness, so many streamers and ribbons are added.

Of the many kite-flyers filling the hills, only three will be awarded prizes. The winner is given a cow and a ride in a sedan chair through the cheering crowd of contestants. Second prize is a pig, and third prize is a sheep. These prizes carry with them the invisible praise and magic of excellence in effort and execution, and the recognition of having the most magic kites in the contest!

HOW TO MAKE A KITE

Supplies you will need (available at most arts and crafts stores):
◆ lightweight paper, 3 feet by 3 feet ◆ 2 round wood dowels (⅛ inch thick); one 36 inches long and one 32 inches long ◆ kite string ◆ thread ◆ glue ◆ twist tab (optional) ◆ paint ◆ scissors ◆ tape ◆ ruler ◆ reinforcement rings (the kind used for notebook binder paper) ◆ crepe paper

▽ 1. Take a lightweight piece of paper that measures 3 feet by 3 feet and lay it on the floor.

△ 2. Paint a big picture on it that can be seen from far away. Remember that your picture can represent a special wish! Let the paint dry.

▽ 3. Now cross the shorter dowel a quarter of the way down the long dowel. (The longer dowel is called the mast, and the point where the two dowels cross is called the joint.)

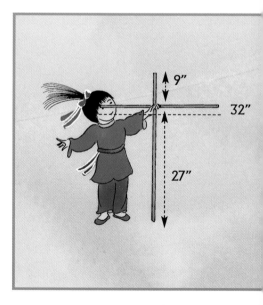

4. Fasten the dowels securely at a right angle with kite string or thread and glue, or with a twist tab.

JOINT

5. Outline the kite with string tied to the four dowel ends. Don't pull the string so tightly that the dowels bend—they should be straight. (Hint: Making a notch at the end of each dowel will help to hold the string in place.)

6. Place your kite frame on the back of your picture, and hold it in place with tape. (Hint: There should be at least 1 inch of paper beyond the frame of your kite.) Trace the outline of your kite on the paper.

7. Make another outline 1 inch wider all around so you can fold the paper over the outlining string, and paste it down. Spaces must be cut in the paper where it matches up to the wood dowels.

8. To attach your flying line, first make two holes in your kite diagonally across the mast: one above the joint, one below the joint—use reinforcements on the holes to prevent the paper from ripping. The string should go through one hole from the front and come back out through the other hole. Tie securely so that the knot is visible from the front of the kite.

9. Adding a tail will help balance the kite so it will fly straight. Cut a hole on each side of the mast, just above the bottom hems of the kite; again, use reinforcements to keep the holes from ripping.

▲ 10. Now you are ready to make the tail. First cut a piece of string that measures 10 feet to 12 feet. Then tie 6-inch crepe-paper bows along the line, one per foot. Now tie the tail string through the holes you made at the bottom of the kite in Step 9.

▲ 11. Stretch the kite tail on the ground. If the wind isn't at least 8 miles per hour, you may need a friend to hold your kite up off the ground to get it airborne.

▲ 12. Run into the wind with your kite behind you. The wind will catch your kite! Let it fly! Let the string out so the kite can go higher—hooray!